A Very Powerful Gift

Author
Pamela Elges Roesler

- Illustrators -
Destyne Richardson
Pamela Elges Roesler

A Very Poweful Gift

Author
Pamela Elges Roesler

- Illustrators -
Destyne Richardson
Pamela Elges Roesler

ARPress
45 Dan Road Suite 5
Canton, MA 02021

Hotline: 1(888) 821-0229
Fax: 1(508) 545-7580

Ordering Information:

Quantity sales. Special discounts are available on quantity purchases by corporations, associations, and others. For details, contact the publisher at the address above.

Printed in the United States of America.

ISBN-13:   Softcover   979-8-89356-800-4
                eBook   979-6-89356-801-1

Library of Congress Control Number: 2024903785

Stewart

could not

find a

reason to

smile.

He looked around.

All his brothers
and
sisters were making
wonderful webs!

4

Their webs were big
with fancy designs.

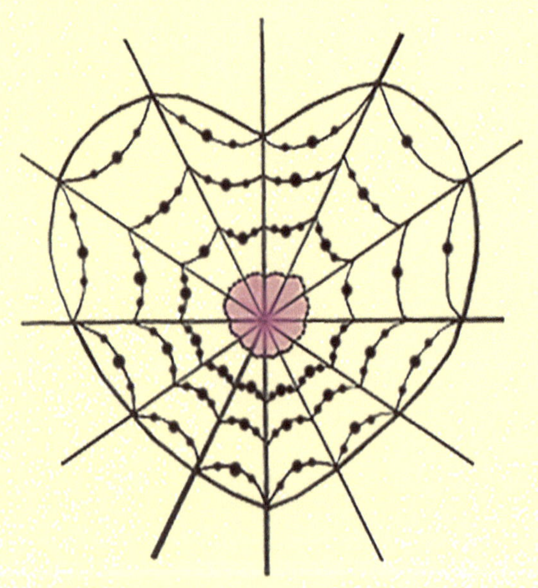

Their webs were
very special.

Stewart's web
was
not very
special.

His web
was
small
and
boring.

Stewart had a serious
problem. He was
afraid to jump.
And . . .

. . . spiders
had to jump
in order to make
fancy webs.

Try as he might,
Stewart
just could
not jump.

His fear was

bigger than

himself!

12

One day,
his mother
gave him
a present.

The box had a special
hat inside,
complete with a
whirligig on top.

14

"This is a magic hat," his mother said. "When you wear it, you will not fall."

"Wear this hat when you jump, and your webs will be beautiful and fancy."

Stewart liked the hat.
It was the color
of the blue sky
and had an
orange whirligig.

This whirligig went 'round and 'round when the air moved.

18

It was a great hat. But . . .
he still wouldn't jump.
He did not trust the hat.

True, it was a fancy hat.
It covered his head and
it did ot fall off.

But Stewart did not feel
any magic when he wore
his new hat.
In fact, he didn't feel any
different at all.

"Wait and see,"
said his mother.

"Just wait and see."

The next morning,
Stewart was awakened
by a lot of noise.

25

BANG!
BOOM!

From his tiny corner
at the top of
the backdoor,
Stewart noticed
a lady with
a large broom.

Stewart was puzzled.
The lady had the broom
upside down.

She was
waving
it
everywhere!

30

Stewart saw
his brother,
sister, and mother
jumping to safety.

Stewart was frozen and could not move.

The lady was coming closer and closer!

The broom
was coming
closer
and
closer!

34

Just as the broom
was
about to hit him,
Stewart
jumped!

He went way up high
and then he
swayed
slowly
down
to
safety.

Stewart landed far away.

And . . .
when he looked up,
he could barely see
his web where he
had been living.

Stewart let out a big sigh
of relief.

"Boy, I sure am glad
I kept my
special hat on
when I fell asleep
last night."

At that moment,
Stewart saw his hat
on the floor,
not far from where
he had landed.

43

The blue hat with an orange
whirlygig had not
helped him at all.

He had done it
all by
himself!

47

Stewart was so proud.

49

His brother, sister, and mother were cheering!

"Yeah!"

"Way to go!"

"Go, Stewart!"

"Wow!
I did it all by myself!
I really jumped!"

"Now I am like all the
other spiders."

52

After the lady with the
broom left, it was
safe to come out.

53

Stewart went over
to get
his special hat.

"Thanks Mom," said Stewart

"It really is a great hat."

"Let's save it just in case there is another spider who is afraid to jump."

The End